A DAY IN THE LIFE OF A BABY GIBBON

A Day in the Life of a Baby Gibbon

by HELEN KAY

pictures by SYMEON SHIMIN

Abelard-Schuman · London · New York · Toronto

© Copyright 1972 · Text by Helen Kay · Illustrations by Symeon Shimin · Library of Congress
Catalogue Card Number: 78-156847 · ISBN: 0 200 71817 7 Trade · 0 200 71818 5 GB ·
Printed in the United States of America

It is so dark under the tall teakwood tree
that you cannot even see the stars.

The large leaves make a thick roof against the sky.

A gibbon family huddles together on the sturdiest limb:
a father, a mother and a baby gibbon.
This is their sleeping tree.

The gibbons, small apes of Thailand, often spend the night
in the leafiest part of this tree.

They can see you—but you can hardly see them.

Can you count the gibbons in the tree?

It is very still in the forest
except for the rustle of the leaves in a breeze or the call
and scurry of the night animals.
Neither the screech of an owl, nor the scampering of
a wide-eyed honey bear awakes the gibbons.

Soon the sun begins to push its way through the wet leaves.
As the night animals go to sleep for the day,
the gibbons wake up.

The father gibbon opens his eyes to the first light.
He stretches his arms that are as long
as his body. He swings to the topmost limb.
He stands as tall as he can for his twenty-four inches
and hoots: "Who, who, who, wah, wah, wah!"

This call wakes up the gibbon world.

Answering shouts come from other gibbon families in the forest.
The morning calls soar and swell and
spread, locating each gibbon family in its home range.
For a deafening moment, as they start the new day,
you would think only gibbons lived here.

In the tree abodes, mother gibbons nurse their infants.
They feed them tiny buds and tender leaves.

Our baby gibbon climbs down two limbs to visit his older brother and sister.
They groom him. They wrestle.
Quickly he runs back to his mother, and watches the young gibbons groom each other.

They are all hungry.
A fruit tree must be found where the family can feed.

They swing out of their tree and, with a leap
and a jump and a dive,
they follow a tree path through the forest.
The father gibbon leads his family over familiar trails.
Father gibbon is a beautiful black—
black as the velvet night, with white-gloved hands
and white-socked feet.
He keeps his family together with his calls.
Other gibbon families hear the sound and know
which way he is going.

The mother gibbon leaps twenty feet
to stand beside the male. Her coat is a soft beige.
She has big brown eyes.
A half-circle fringe of white hair
frames her black face.
She waits for the baby to catch up.

The downy-haired baby gibbon is as black as his father.
He has a white ruff around his face
and over his eyebrows.
He is already too heavy to be carried.
His mother no longer lets him cling—like the
smallest infants who hold tight to their mothers' hips
with two thin arms—while she swings
and leaps and runs along the treetop path.
The baby gibbon must keep up with his mother on his own.

He stays very close to her.
He will not lose sight of her as she moves,
nor she of him. When she crouches,
he crouches. When she leaps, he takes small jumps behind her.
Then she waits for him.

The other gibbons race ahead.
All together now, they climb and swing and jump and leap.
At the end of their range, in the full sun,
stands a ripening plum tree.

The purple fruit is almost within reach.

Suddenly there are other gibbon voices—loud and near.

Our gibbon group stops.
Other gibbons are on their way to the same plum tree.
Who will get there first?

Our leader waits.

Now both groups are face to face.
They shout and call.
The cries of the mothers behind them add to the noise.
The sound is so loud it frightens the baby gibbon.
He clings to his mother.
The young gibbons jump up and down and shout.
The baby gibbon calls, too.
It is just a screech.
One day he will have a big voice like his father's.

The gibbons can be heard by the rice farmers
in the field at the edge of the forest.
The farmers dig deeper.
They believe that gibbon calls will help their plants
grow tall and yield good grain.

Both gibbon groups want the ripe fruit from the same plum tree.
Which gibbon group will get them?
The gibbon leader who looks the fiercest?
The one who shouts the loudest?
The group with the most gibbons?
The gibbons with the longest teeth?

No, none of these . . . today.

Then who will go away?

The first gibbon group moves forward.
This plum tree is in *their* range.

The second group moves in another direction.
The forest is large.
They will find another plum tree, or a nut tree,
or even a fig tree in their own range.

The path is open now.
The noise stops.
The gibbon acrobats leap and tumble even faster.
They run and dive.
Now up a tree, now on the ground,
almost flying through the air.
One last burst of speed, and they are in the plum tree.
It is a big tree, full of fruit.
The plums are soft and tart, and, oh, so sweet.

Carefully the gibbons pluck each plum.
The mother peels one
and the small gibbon eats it from her hands.
Then he peels his own.
Then another and another.
Soon there are no ripe plums left.

The sun is high and very hot.

Beyond the plum tree is a shady grove.
Here they stop to rest.
There is no more shouting or calling.
Father naps in a tree.
So does the baby gibbon beside his mother.
The leaves stir gently, but the gibbons are all very still.

Our downy-haired gibbon is the first to move.
He finds a vine and wakes his older brother. Each pulls
at an end. When the bigger gibbon gets the vine,
the baby runs and hides behind his sister.
They race and leap around, until exhausted.
Then they sit down and quietly groom each other.
Soon the hottest part of the day has passed.

When the gibbon male has finished his nap, he rises.
So does the whole group.
They move on to find more berries, buds and tender greens.
They snack and dawdle as they wander
all afternoon until sunset.

It gets dark in the forest very quickly.

The gibbons move faster. They are searching
for another tree in which to spend the night.
The baby gibbon runs beside his mother.
Together, they leap from limb to limb,
from tree to tree...faster...faster...
Suddenly there is a wide chasm between the trees.

First the father leaps across.
The mother jumps and joins him.
The other young gibbons follow.
But the smallest gibbon cannot make the jump.
The downy hairs on his head bristle with fear.
He screams and whines.

His mother waits for him. She calls.

He runs to the edge.
He backs away. He cannot cross that open space.
He sits and cries—without tears.

The mother gibbon comes back to him.
He puts his arms around her hips.
But he is too big to be carried.
Instead, with her feet, the mother holds the limb
on which they both are sitting.
She stretches her hands across and grabs the limb
on the far side. She holds it tight,
and she does not release her foothold either.
She has bridged the gap.
Now her body is a bridge for the baby gibbon.

The little ape runs across
her stretched back—to the other side.

They are on their way again, together.

At their next tree abode,
the gibbons scamper up the largest limb,
in the leafiest part of the tree, and huddle:
the father, the mother and the baby gibbon.

Below them, on another limb, sit the two younger gibbons.

The forest darkens beneath the still light sky.
The thick leaves hide the glow of the setting sun.
Soon they are all asleep.
The honey bear and the wide-eyed owl wake up, but
the night animals do not rouse the gibbons.

Can you see the sleeping gibbons in the dark?

Tomorrow when the sun comes up—another day
will come to the gibbon forest,
just like the day that passed—unless it rains.

Then they will sit all day, curled up like balls
to keep dry, and stay very quiet.

ABOUT THE AUTHOR
Helen Kay is the author of more than a dozen books
for children, including the popular
A DUCK FOR KEEPS, AN EGG IS FOR WISHING
and A LION FOR A SITTER.
A former researcher for *Time* and *Fortune,*
she edited trade papers for several years before
turning to writing for children.
Helen Kay is married, the mother of three children,
and lives in New York City.

ABOUT THE ARTIST
Symeon Shimin was born in Russia and came to
the United States at the age of ten.
He attended classes at Cooper Union, but received
his real art training in the museums and
galleries of Europe. In 1938, Mr. Shimin was chosen
to paint a mural in the Department of Justice Building
in Washington, D.C., and since that time his work
has been exhibited extensively
in the United States. He is the illustrator
of many wonderful books for children.